Cont

The Devil Book

ASTA OLIVIA
NORDENHOF

Translated from the Danish by Caroline Waight

JONATHAN CAPE
LONDON

1 3 5 7 9 10 8 6 4 2

Jonathan Cape, an imprint of Vintage, is part of the
Penguin Random House group of companies

Vintage, Penguin Random House UK, One Embassy
Gardens, 8 Viaduct Gardens, London SW11 7BW

penguin.co.uk/vintage
global.penguinrandomhouse.com

First published in Great Britain with the title *The Devil Book* by
Jonathan Cape in 2025
First published in Denmark with the title *Djævlebogen* by Gads Forlag in 2023

Typeset in 11.6/15.8pt Minion Pro by Six Red Marbles UK, Thetford, Norfolk
Printed and bound in Great Britain by Clays Ltd, Elcograf S.p.A.

The authorised representative in the EEA is Penguin Random House
Ireland, Morrison Chambers, 32 Nassau Street, Dublin D02 YH68

A CIP catalogue record for this book is available from the British Library

ISBN 9781787335189

Foreword

LOLLAND, 6 November 2022

Readers of volume I in this series
will remember
that the story ended
with a call
from Copenhagen
it was T
ringing
T the businessman
who had plans
to start
a shipping corporation
and was trying to find
investors
in this volume, II,
we were supposed
to follow him
from childhood up until
the night
when he sat waiting for
the news that
the fire
on the *Scandinavian Star*

had successfully been
set
I wrote three versions
of that book
and hated
every one
what was I doing
in
that man's
head
there was nothing
to be found there
if I say
that he
like others
is prepared
to kill
for profit
then I've said of him
what there is to be said
and can content myself
with
adding: yes
he was a person too
he had
a phone with a very
long antenna
and a mother
whose lifelong pain
was that
she'd given birth to him

so I had to
put the owner
in the grave
and instead begin
to try to find
the father of
the modern businessman
this happened just
as the pandemic
was called off
for the third time
planes returning
to the sky
it made me
so angry
who
I asked
who
has persuaded us
that happiness is
doing the impossible
it was
the genius the
lunatic
the original
burner of forests
so the fourth book
I wrote
was about Christopher Columbus
he sailed of course
across the Atlantic

could barely
keep a salted sardine down
for sheer excitement
over this potentially
wildly lucrative
contract
and the trade winds
they were his fluke scoop
the trade winds brought him
and his rotting ship
led them
to another world
where he tramped around in heavy
Spanish boots
and wondered
what a colourful bird
might go for
on the European market
since it had never
been sold before
so he began to murder
kidnap kids
put people
up for sale
but don't think
he took pleasure in it
no, it was
a tremendous
bother
really, he simply calculated
it might

pay off
500 years later
the *Scandinavian Star* arose
in the middle of the Caribbean Sea
the sails replaced
by a large
hot engine
she was a floating
casino for the white
American middle class
then she was bought
by a Dane
sailed back
across the Atlantic
set alight
but that
manuscript
I also hated
believe me when I tell you
I practically threw up
every time I opened the document
in such cases
when you've lost
yourself
when with fierce disdain
you force yourself
to read yet another
biography of Columbus
or another
article
about a shipowner who got away

with murder
in cases such as those you've got to ask yourself
what was my motto
again?
my motto
which I had forgotten
in my struggle
to write a
proper book
about the inner life
of great men
my motto
is as follows
it's a simple one and
good:
fuck men!
when I came to think
about it
I came to think
that I
can do
whatever I want
so this
is my book
this is
for you
this is
an erotic thriller
about businessmen and
the devil
there are

some poems
about love
a speech
from the asylum
it will be your job
to make it fit
into the series
I mean really
I can't
do the whole thing
by myself

Asta Olivia Nordenhof

The Devil in a High-Rise

Day 1

It's raining in London. I'm in quarantine with a man I met the other day on a trip from Copenhagen to Vejle. A series of bureaucratic hiccups at Kastrup Airport had prevented him from picking up the rental car he'd booked from home, and so he'd had to take the train, like me. They were running a replacement bus service, as they so often do, and among the little group of people mutely waiting to be picked up outside Korsør Station, he stood out by virtue of a loud telephone conversation. I'd noticed him and his fitted navy blue suit and bright white trainers, but he must have slipped my mind again, because it came as a surprise to find him standing right beside me. 'A train that's actually a bus, it's a contradiction in terms,' he said, and smiled a practised, quickly cut-short smile before adding he had noticed me back at the main station.

We sat next to each other on the bus, and as it drove we carried on an undramatic conversation. He was recently divorced, and talked to me about his failed marriage, about why, in his opinion, they had split (his wife didn't understand him). He also talked about his job, which was the reason for his visit to Denmark. He worked as a programming architect, a title he assumed required further explanation, and when I confirmed that assumption, he launched into a lengthy story about ATMs and the system behind them, a story I listened to with interest but am not capable of reproducing here.

I lied, as usual, about who I am. When I was younger I'd think up extravagant lies, but as I age my stories have become more plausible and frankly dull. Even so, I outdid myself this time: I was a journalist at one of the country's major dailies, and had recently published a polemical book about declining educational standards – don't ask me how I came up with something *that* tedious. Several times during my explanation, my fellow passenger gave me a look of what felt like almost digital precision, a scan I enjoyed being put through.

It turned out we were both headed for Vejle, and only after we'd exchanged a quick hug outside the station and gone our separate ways did it occur to me that our entire conversation had been spoken sotto voce, almost at a whisper, as though we both knew instantly we were sharing a secret.

When I got to the hotel room where I was due to spend the night, I went to sit out on the balcony. There was a smell of wet trees, sour earth and night. I had the same quivering sense of my phone's nearness that I imagine a dog might have, even in sleep, for the bone its paw is resting on, and sure enough it wasn't long before I had a text. He'd never travel on the Danish national railway again, he said, but it had been a pleasure meeting me.

The following night we met again in Copenhagen. I suggested a hotel bar I'd never been to before, and introduced it as my regular. I like it here, I said, I like to feel anonymous, which strictly speaking I suppose was true.

We sat down on a group of peculiarly low sofas, and he told me more about his abortive marriage. When her dad fell ill, his wife had insisted they buy a house just a few doors down from her parents. He had moved like a ghost through that house, where more and more his wife (not explicitly, but in demeanour) had demanded he transform, and stand in for the father who was disappearing. 'Well,' I said, and raised my eyebrows, before – showing little sensitivity to what he'd just told me – I took the conversation in a more theoretical direction.

'Fundamentally I don't believe in marriage. It would never work for me, anyway,' I said, and elaborated: 'I can be monogamous, sure, even though it doesn't really come naturally to me, I have no trouble being considerate. But I can't miss people, and that's the problem. If a man is gone, he's gone, and I don't miss him. I completely forget that he was ever there. The minute he's out the door, BAM, my slate is clean. I don't know how they sense it, men, but they do, they know they've been forgotten, and it baffles them and makes them doubt the kind of person that I am.' That's what I said, and after a contrived pause I added, in a tone meant to suggest thoughtfulness, that maybe I *was* a little bit callous. It was a gamble, but I could tell it got him even more intrigued – leaning forward in his seat he took my hand, and gave it a quick squeeze. 'I don't think so.'

We had another glass of wine, engaged in each other's lives in the same hospitable and blithe way as before, then parted outside the hotel, with a hug almost as fleeting as the one in Vejle.

The next day he sent me a picture he'd taken outside Heathrow. It was of a wet dog on a lead, presumably connected to a human being, although the picture cut it off before it reached the person. The dog was soaked, and looked like it regretted everything about its life. *I'm this dog without you*, he texted, and in the message that immediately followed: *You should come to London!*

I must admit (although I like to think of myself as someone unsurprisable) that this surprised me. Under the current restrictions, as soon as I arrived in England I'd have to quarantine for a fortnight in his flat. *Sure*, I replied promptly, and to emphasise that I wasn't being ironic, I sent another text: *No seriously, I'm coming!*

True, I felt a certain interest in this impulsive Londoner, and I was intrigued to learn whether he was fibbing about his life too, and if he knew that I had; but that wasn't really why I accepted. For years now I'd been trying in vain to write a novel about a person I used to know, a man called T, and when the invitation came I felt with animal certainty that this was just the setting I'd been waiting for.

*

Over the next twenty-four hours we sorted out the paper-work each of us had to sign, solemnly declaring that we were engaged and could therefore request to see each other despite the various travel restrictions.

Then I flew, whisking over several countries and across the sea, passed through various checkpoints at Heathrow, and was freed at last into a hall where my host was waiting for me. We walked tensely and without a word towards the car park, and in that vast space, cold as church, I felt among the glossy black cars quite happy.

And now here I am. I told my host I've got an important project to finish during my stay. I asked for his under-standing, since I'd be so busy with work, and he gave it to me unreservedly. He was even kind enough to put a table and chair by the window, so when I lift my eyes from the computer I can gaze out at the Thames. It's raining, and it's been dark for ages. Tomorrow I will wake up and write about T.

Day 2

I woke early this morning, having forgotten about my host. I remembered he existed when I rolled onto my side and saw his back, which pulsed as the air we were sharing circulated through his body. I didn't want to disturb him, so I pulled a jumper over my nightie as quietly as possible and crept out onto the balcony. I stood there for a while, letting the damp, inaccessible city hold my heart, until suddenly it occurred to me I should be freezing. I looked down at my bare feet to assure myself they were still there, and decided I appeared to be alive.

When I came back into the bedroom the bed was made, the only evidence of my host's recent presence a faint floral note in the air. Sitting on the edge of the bed, I became aware of a note on the bedside table. *See you later*, it said. Below the words was a heart, a childish doodle so offensive to me that I couldn't help but giggle.

Still, if there's one talent I do have, it's for a swift forgetting, and by the time I went into the living room I'd already put my giddiness behind me. It didn't seem the least bit strange that my host had put a croissant on my desk, on the contrary; I swallowed it with distracted impatience, then switched on my laptop and stared at it until it went to sleep, switched it on again and let it hibernate again.

It's been more than ten years since I left T with a suitcase full of cash in my possession. I no longer know the young woman who went with him, but then again, did I ever know myself? Had I not simply bobbed along on the incomprehensible current of money? In any case, what's kept me from writing our story isn't my suspicion that T is a devil, it's more the question: if T *is* a devil, what does that make me?

But I can't put off the story any longer. I've made sure of that by planting myself here, in this high-rise apartment block. The architecture of quarantine is the setting within which the story can and must be told.

*

It was 2009, shortly after Lehman Brothers had collapsed and the world's economy had gone up in flames. I mention it here because Steffie mentioned it to me, during my job interview at Velvet Deluxe. 'Sales of luxury goods nosedive in times of crisis,' she said, 'and obviously that affects us too.' The money wasn't what it used to be, but I could count on making a decent living, for sure. 'That's okay,' I said, as I took from my bag the underwear I was going to be photographed in.

Throughout the session that followed, Steffie instructed me matter-of-factly and in the imperative. Lean over the bed, cup a hand around your breast, and so on. Afterwards, she transferred the images to her computer and showed me the ones she was planning to use online. We were just weighing up the pros and cons of a photo where my legs looked nice and long but my arse appeared a little flat when, all of a sudden, Steffie turned away from the screen and looked at me. 'This work isn't for everyone,' she said. There was something prosaic about Steffie that I instantly admired, a dauntless love of facts, in this case the fact that some people will be crushed by life while others cope. 'I get that,' I said, 'but I'd like to try it.'

I'd decided long before then to start working as a prosti-tute. I had seen a number of places and had chosen Velvet

Deluxe purely because I liked its interior the best. It was pink and red, floral and gold, it was silly and OTT in a way I much preferred to the professional whites and dentist-dreary orchids I'd seen elsewhere.

I had made the decision – to become a prostitute, that is – on the way home from a meeting at the benefits office, where the lady behind the glass carapace explained to me that my weekly payment had been halved due to some reform or other that had recently come in. Suicide or prostitution, I thought on the way home; but this isn't a victim story.

This is a story about how the government can go fuck themselves, and anyway, I'd always liked the idea of making a quick buck.

I was mentally ill at the time, whatever that means, but at any rate I was mostly incapable of socially acceptable behaviour. I flirted with everybody, I cried at the slightest provocation or laughed when I needed to be serious. Think of a foamy sponge; you wring and wring but all you get is dirty water. Long story short, I wasn't particularly charming, but I was clever, and I was beautiful, and since nobody cared about the former, I intended to exploit the latter to the full.

It struck me as an advantage that the sex industry was considered immoral. The thought that I was taking part in an immoral enterprise helped allay my fear of failure and judgement. How much more wrong could you go, once you'd reached the bottom of the barrel? Then there was the money, which far exceeded what I could have earned in other unskilled jobs, and the way they gave it to you in an envelope at shift's end, the way you didn't have to wait, that appealed to me as well.

So I told Steffie I wanted to get started. Also, that I knew what my name was going to be.

'Daphne?' She eyed me quizzically.

'It's from Greek mythology. Daphne turned herself into a tree to escape the love of a man.'

While I've been writing, my host has come home. I've been typing even harder at my keyboard, to let him know I'm on a mission that requires my full attention. But my instinctive anger towards him was evidently unnecessary. He simply left me alone, not bothering me with so much as a hello. Now the aroma of browning thyme drifts in from the kitchen. I could write that 'I love him'. It wouldn't be true, but it's not necessarily untrue either. If I lived here long enough, there would come a point when I said it. Half as a formality, to justify my continued presence, and half to acknowledge that he'd become a not-insignificant habit, and to ask if I'd also grown indispensable to him.

Day 3

Last night when I couldn't sleep, I felt like counting something. Count those you love, I told myself, and quick as lightning I went through them in my head, those to whom I can give nothing any more, and from whom I refuse to receive anything. Of a crumpled car we say it's written off; a person in the same state we call a psychopath. Shall I unfold, and love again? I wondered, pulse rising at the thought, palms sweaty.

I don't know how I finally got to sleep, but I dreamed of a duck that wouldn't leave me alone, and which weighed down my movements to such an extent that in the end I sought help at a disused hospital, where I'd heard some doctors had barricaded themselves on the top floor.

Unlike the day before, my host was already gone by the time I woke up, and on tenterhooks I glanced towards the bedside table: yes, he'd left another heart. You've got to understand, I've been alone a while, I'm easily stirred up, and I have to be on guard against this weakness of mine.

I swallowed the croissant and anxiously opened the world processor, by means of which I must summon myself forth.

*

My days at the brothel flowed like oil, until T arrived. My mind was slow, very elastic. Not until winter came did it occur to me that it must have been summer, that until lately the roses had given off their dizzying, incestuous perfume in the courtyard garden outside Velvet Deluxe.

*

I was popular, with a steady stream of clients. Fourteen on my first shift. When I woke up the next day, I was very muscle-sore and acutely rich. I spent all the money in a single shopping trip, my nerves bristling up against the world like needles. And on it went. Show up, men, trips up and down the main drag as though on an electric wire. I drank a lot. That wasn't new, but in those days the hangovers were a marvellous, white-wine-dulled membrane between me and the world.

Only a few clients stand out in my memory now. They made themselves noteworthy by wanting something a little out of the ordinary, I suppose. There was the Japanese game designer who was in Copenhagen for a few months, the only one who ever asked me to say I loved him. There was the one called Poul, who I remember because he was always careful to book the first slot on my shifts, and because he alone among my clients I think I hated. He liked me to come in in flat shoes, and preferably in my regular clothes. My regular clothes weren't very sexy, I objected, but he told me I had no idea what he found sexy, and that was true, of course. I remember him once bringing in an empty roll of loo paper and asking me to put it on his dick, to tell him it was smaller and more pathetic than the roll. There was the one with the gigantic cock, who'd given up on a normal sex life. At the brothel you could expect professionalism, which meant that his member was subject to neither ridicule nor complaint. Then there were the herds. The boys who came in groups of three or four, one of them usually a virgin. His lot was to frighten and humiliate himself in front of his whooping friends, groping and fumbling, so that afterwards he could call himself a man.

Mostly, I was on shift with Anastacia. We only knew each other's working names, and wouldn't have dreamed of asking for identifiable details. Anastacia had long black hair with an extraordinary sheen. She knew everything there was to know about products that could bring a shine to hair and nails and skin. On shift she always brought in a wonderfully thick and downy duvet, and occasionally, when we were both on our break, she lifted it up and told me to lie next to her. Together, under the duvet, we watched whatever afternoon programming happened to be on. We watched *Ally McBeal*, *Friends*, that show about the lawyer and the hippie who move in together, and the one where the girl lives with her screwball single mum. When it came to *Beverly Hills*, we both liked Valerie the best, or rather, we hated all the others. The strangest series was *Melrose Place*. The storyline never really went anywhere; it felt more like a funnel. The characters were always by a pool, hemmed in by a tall apartment block, and it was as though they could never really get to anywhere else.

Anastacia couldn't understand why I wasn't – or did not at least become – a lesbian. 'WHY?' she exclaimed one day, pointing at Steve from *Beverly Hills* onscreen before jabbing her extended index finger into my ribs. 'Is that really what you want??' Not that she personally was interested, as she frequently reminded me: she thought I seemed like *a proper little princess*, but then some people were into that, as she said. She understood even less how I could actually come

20

when I was with a client. 'You little whore! You actually come! You are SO fucked up, sweetie!' she crowed one day when I came back into the break room. She must have overheard my orgasm through the wall. I got the sense she thought it was so unheard-of, so utterly bananas, that she genuinely liked me for it.

And she was right, I did come. I didn't even need to use the lube that was always on the bedside table – it happened of its own accord. In fact, I've never had orgasms before or since like the ones I had at Velvet Deluxe. Not sure what to make of that. I know I was alive, that the days passed; it's hard to say much else. It was a life, and somehow it was mine. Then T came along and took me on his journey. I promise I'll write about that part tomorrow, I'm too tired now.

Day 4

Continued rain in London. Nonetheless, my host is out on his rollerblades. I'm not trying to be funny, that's actually what he's doing. He rollerblades every day, work permitting, but at the moment he's hampered by the exercise restrictions, which allow Londoners one hour of physical activity a day within a radius of three kilometres from their own home. He just manages to reach the Thames before he has to turn back.

That information all came out last night, when I agreed to share a bottle of wine with him. I must admit, the new haircut my host's barber gave him had a euphoric effect on me. It put me in a laughing mood, and in that state he got me to say yes.

Still, I stuck to my principle of mainly listening (people shouldn't be so ready to blurt things out and give themselves away, not when they know perfectly well what the cost can be), and he was only too happy to talk, in his usual affable and discreet way. And so I learned about not just his passion for rollerblading but also various bygone aspirations, which he had stifled when he realised that if he kept pursuing them he could kiss goodbye to making money. He had tried his hand at acting, then for several years he'd been the lead singer in a band that almost made it big with their Christmas song (he played it for me). True to tradition, it was about putting your differences aside and loving others. But since not even this short-lived success had produced any significant change in his financial situation, he had decided to remake his life entirely, studying first business and later programming. I listened, happy as a sleepwalker, not quite able to believe we were actually in the same place, that we were ostensibly living and connected.

The plan is for me to introduce T today. I think I'm afraid, that must be what the faint tingle in my fingers means. But why? What could I possibly write that would appal me? Or is it the other way around? Do I already know I cannot be appalled? Is it simply that there is no depth behind the screen I call my life? Will I go on with my dialogue each day, blithely unaware of the madman who implanted it in me?

*

It was a day like any other when T entered Velvet Deluxe. The woman who worked the phones must have met him at the door and shown him to a room, she must have told me I had a client. I must have got up off the sofa, cast a swift look in the mirror and fixed my make-up, then – riding on an anxious, cash-drunk high – opened the door and found T in the armchair.

I might have noticed he was good-looking and elegantly dressed. Maybe I was slightly relieved that he appeared well groomed. On the other hand, I'd had quite a lot of clients by then and preferred not to form much impression of them. They were who they were. It wasn't any of my business.

It wasn't in itself unusual that T said nothing, or that he made no move to get up from his chair. He was far from my first uneasy customer. My job consisted mostly of assuaging guilt; or, more accurately, of being the stage on which guilt could be proclaimed and the hard surface from which it resonated back. So it was routine for me to sit down on the bed, to smile sympathetically and pat the mattress, to show that he didn't have to feel awkward about coming to get what he'd paid for, but when he still didn't move, an unfamiliar discomfort started to creep up on me. You can be a performing bear and take a certain pleasure in giving the idiots what they want, but if you're led onstage and sense that nothing further is required . . .

He must be very shy, I insisted to myself, although nothing about his body language suggested awkwardness. Far from it. His expression was composed and open as he watched me, as though I were a small, twitching germ under a microscope and he a scientist, seeing the greatness in his otherwise unprepossessing discovery.

Very shy, I decided, and stood up to approach him, but he raised his hand to stop me coming closer and pointed instead at the armchair opposite his. When I sat down, he reached out and gave my hand a forceful squeeze. 'T,' he said. 'You're just what I've been looking for.'

For a moment I was sure he must have come straight from the psych ward, that he'd been let out for a few hours unaccompanied, probably for the first time in a while, but then he went on.

'I'm going on a trip tomorrow, and I've been looking for the right companion. Now I'm delighted to discover that it's you. I pay well, but in return you agree to be told no more about the job than what I've just explained. You are not permitted to ask questions, now or ever, but you may withdraw from the agreement at any time. Simply say you wish to leave, and from that moment you're relieved of duty. You're looking a little slack-jawed, I see, but I know as well as you do it's an affectation. You've been dreaming of this moment – waiting for just such a chance as this. You're beautiful, but there are plenty of others more beautiful, so don't think that's why I'm taking you. What I need is someone with a pure heart, which is to say someone entirely without conscience. Most people would rather not see themselves that way, but I know you're not most people. I'd like to hear from you tonight. For the sake of ritual, let's pretend I don't already know your answer. Here, why don't you take my card?'

T, that was all it said, and a telephone number. By the time I looked back up from the card, he had already left.

'So?' Anastacia asked when I came back into the break-room. Evidently she could tell something was different. I shrugged, sat down, and went through the motions of watching a sitcom, which was about a gay man living with the woman he was supposed to marry. What was going through my mind? Hard to explain. Think of a storm inside a large and empty hall. That same night, I called and took the job.

Day 5

This is the first chance I've had to sit down at my laptop all day. I thought I was disciplined, that I was work ethic incarnate, but apparently I'm easily seduced into idleness. You only have to suggest it to me.

It's all because my host had a day off. He doesn't do weekends – days off come without warning, a meeting cancelled or postponed, and a period of time is created in which he can focus on his interests and relationships.

'I'd like to invite my siblings round to lunch,' he announced in a calm, authoritative voice, as though he knew very well I was happy to let the workspace he'd offered me be repurposed as a family zone.

I watched from the balcony as he set off down the road to undertake one of the activities still allowed by law: food shopping.

He returned home with mushrooms, a beautifully striped squash and some cold, bloated celery, the flavour of which he thought could be brought out by frying it in butter for a long time on a low heat.

I offered to help with the preparations, but only as a formality. I understand that he wants to perform his life for me, just the way he's dreamed it. My role is to enjoy the show. To take delivery.

His siblings looked a lot like him, their ages similarly difficult to guess. The suit and button-down shirt seemed to be a family uniform. I did my best not to laugh at the sight of the three pairs of chalk-white trainers now lined up in the hall. What a strange adventure this is, I thought, as I followed the cheery siblings into the living room. I soon saw that they preferred to formulate all statements as jokes, and joined in as they laughed elegantly about the pandemic and the absurdities it threw up, such as my voluntary confinement with their brother.

*

The food was largely ready, with the exception of the lemon sauce, which had to be made moments before serving. My host was practically hovering in the kitchen as he opened the crémant, stirred the sauce, grated the lemon zest. Meanwhile, I had trouble striking the right pose. Should I lean against a kitchen cupboard? Sit on the floor, or on one of the stools by the kitchen island? It's a peculiar defect I've developed since seducing men professionally. Every now and then, I suddenly find myself doubting how it all works, if somehow you're also meant to be yourself. Without the money as a guideline, without the list of services and the contract, you're left fluttering, a woman alleged. I struggled with myself for a few agonising minutes, constantly shifting my grip on the champagne glass, sat down and stood up again, until I remembered that the solution is always to listen. The conversation was about *ghost ships*, the infected cruise liners which, when the pandemic hit, were turned away from all the ports and left to drift at sea. 'I thought,' my host laughed, 'that would be that. If it wasn't Judgement Day, it was certainly the end of the cruise industry. But now look. People set off again at the end of the summer like they couldn't imagine it would run them into trouble.'

I'd been knocking back the crémant, and was already tipsy by the time we sat down at the table. I don't know when I last allowed myself to drink. I'd forgotten how wonderfully loose you get, the body falling off its own story like well-cooked chicken falls off the bone. We passed the vegetables around, praising their appearance and aroma, and laughed at my host's anecdote about his encounter with a stray dog. It had popped up in the middle of the street, snarling at him ominously, and being armed with nothing but an organic cabbage he'd just bought at the farmers' market, he felt obliged to throw it. The dog snatched it in mid-air, clamping down with such force that it couldn't get its teeth back out. It stood there enraged, shaking the magnificent specimen in its mouth, while my host set off at a run.

Maybe it was the bubbly clouding my wits, but the way I heard it, his siblings asked me a question in unison, as though in a choir: 'What do people eat for lunch in Denmark?' I suppressed a smile. I knew I was about to score a point. 'Herring in a curry sauce piled on bread.' It landed as expected: everybody laughed and offered condolences, but then my host decided to up the ante by remarking that in addition to having survived Danish cuisine, I also happened to be a writer. That flustered me. 'No, no,' I said instinctively, before I remembered this was precisely what I'd told him. 'Well, yes,' I added, 'but who wants to talk about work when you can talk about herring?'

I can't explain how I got this far into my stay before realising my host could look me up online, and might with the assistance of Google Translate figure out that while I was indeed a writer, I wasn't the polemic-penning kind, and I certainly wasn't the daughter of a famous textile manufacturer whose ambitions for me I'd defied by becoming a flight attendant in my early twenties. Nor had I spent several years living an easy life in the skies then several more in a party town, until I lost my taste for debauchery, went home, and trained as a journalist.

I glanced around at the shirt-wearing sibling clones. They radiated elegant, haughty indulgence. Well, I thought, if they all know I'm lying, if it entertains them to give me rope to hang myself while I sit here thinking how audacious I am, then I've got to hand it to them, it's well played. My discomfort turned to excitement. I clutched my glass and raised it to new friendships. Now the battle had begun in earnest.

But how I battled – what happened during the rest of lunch – has mysteriously slipped my mind. There's just a gap, a shaft after the toast that leads directly to the hall, where we stood, my host and I, and said goodbye like an old married couple. His hand brushed my hip, and I remembered a display at the aquarium that showed how much electricity the electric eel was currently producing. It would be easy to conclude that what I felt was lust, or maybe even love. But you've got to remember, I'd been repressing that part of myself for a long time. Imagine going down into the larder and picking up a jam jar, lifting the lid to discover that somebody – and it can only be you, it's your handwriting on the label – made cherry compote many years before. Wouldn't you be surprised? Wouldn't you think: Hang on, what's this? What was I thinking? That I'd eat it? Really?

My host had just opened another bottle of wine when suddenly his day off was interrupted by the sound of his phone. 'I've got to go,' he said, after a quick glance at the screen, and I have to admit that I was struck by a hard, ringing feeling when he shut the door behind him. I must have wanted him to stay.

Now I stare instead at my laptop, by means of which I must pass judgement once again on who I am.

*

From the moment T made his offer, a tether ran from me to him, and that tether was the only thing I cared about in all the world. When we spoke on the phone, briefly, he specified that I was to pack light. Phones were not allowed. No reading material. No music. I could not tell anyone that I was leaving. Just as well – the only people I saw regularly (apart from my clients) were Anastacia and the lady on reception. It wouldn't be the first time a person whose real name they didn't know missed a shift and was never heard from again. I thought briefly of Poul. Would he replace me immediately with someone else, or did he believe we had a special connection? He had said once, with his dick inside me and his eyes on mine, that I had what it took to go to university, that I should have taken that path. Was it a fetish, when he said that stuff, and could he act it out with anyone that had a face, and a hole for him to come in?

Not long ago I'd moved into my dad's old flat. Now I lay in the bed where he had lately died and stared up at the ceiling, where a pattern made of gaffer tape was meant to mask the cracks and stop the plaster sprinkling down. I followed the lines of the black and silver work of art, trying to find the points of intersection. I wanted to be beautiful when I showed up at the airport the next morning, and since sleep beautifies, I wanted to fall asleep. But it was hopeless. An hour and a half later I had to face the fact that I was about to burst, the way I think of a flower bud before it splits to make room for its hard-pressed leaves.

I made the rest of the night pass by figuring out how to comply with his instructions to pack light. I had no idea what the climate might be like where we were going, nor anything about what we were to do there. But it didn't matter – the sets of thermals and practical shoes I laid out on the floor were just for show. I knew very well that in the end I would choose solely on the basis of what looked sexy. At Velvet Deluxe I'd landed on a romantic aesthetic. Muted tones and light make-up, ruffles and lace, but nothing too overdone. I appealed to clients who preferred to think of their desires as high-end natural. But it was different showing up fully clothed, rather than cutting straight to underwear. I tried on countless options, but ultimately it came down to two: a serious, armoured one consisting of a black, knee-length, form-fitting jacket with sharp shoulders and high, shiny black boots with silver buckles; and a youthful, trashy one – a gold-coloured biker jacket, hotpants, nylon stockings and ankle boots with stiletto heels.

At seven a.m. I got onto the metro in the gold jacket and rode it to the airport. I looked around at the other passengers, grumpily awake or still cocooned in tiredness, and felt I'd left the world they moved in. They were beautiful, iconically melancholy, with their takeaway coffee cups and downcast eyes. They bore witness to their era with a sacro-sanct naivety, as do all relics of the past. Of course I was afraid of what awaited me, but it was a wondrous fear. It seemed to bear me forward on a throne.

At the arrivals hall, I found T where he said he'd be. He wore a grey suit. It was a bit outmoded, large and eighties-ish and very beautiful. 'I'm going to say it's a hen do, just so you know,' he said, taking a sleep mask and headphones out of his bag. He drew the mask down over my eyes and put the head-phones on me. Bizarrely, he'd chosen to play me *Abba Gold*.

With my skull full of Abba's thinly energetic Swedish disco and an utterly sensational, physical point of concentration building in my right shoulder, where he'd placed his hand, I let myself be guided through the airport. What was hap-pening around us, I don't know. I imagine the airport staff laughing dutifully on being informed that they were wit-nessing the start of a hen do. In any case, we got on board the plane, which felt both narrower and more fragile when you couldn't see it. T led me down the aisle and pressed me into a seat. Then the plane took off. There was a light wind, a horror that rose from the belly to the head before it was lost to the sky.

Day 7

I'm in quarantine in London, for the seventh day now. It's raining.

*

Yesterday I didn't write at all. My host did not return from his sudden evening meeting, and I woke to the absence of a heart on the bedside table. It shook me, I must admit, the missingness of it running like an awl through my internal organs. I thought I'd weaned myself off hope. But now here I was hoping, and to cover up the shock, maybe, I had to overwrite the hope with paranoia.

Why had my host appeared on that high-speed train? Why did he say he'd noticed me at the main station? Did he know it was me he was looking for, and if so, why? How could I believe that he, who was handsome, who had money, would fling his impulsive love at scum like me? I replayed the day before, the meeting with his siblings, the message that took him abruptly away from me, and all of a sudden it seemed tightly choreographed, as though other people had been watching on, whispering how the scene should be played.

If fear is a horse, a great heavy-muscled sharp-accelerating beast, then I'd kept it tightly reined for many years, a demented, smothered charger at my core, but now it tore loose, now the shabby creature bolted in a frenzy. Heart pounding, fingers abuzz, I set about ransacking the flat for some sort of proof that it was a person, not an agent, I was living with.

But there was no sign of life. Everything was empty. The kitchen cupboards were empty, apart from the crockery we had used. No forgotten, superfluous appliances, no straggling collection of Tupperware, no corny porcelain set accepted out of guilt because an aunt said before she died she wanted you to have it. It was empty. And everything – it struck me now – was suspiciously clean. Not a speck of dust, not a spot of grease to be found.

Head swimming, I threw my things into my bag. It wasn't a person but an algorithm that had furnished this home, kitting it out with just the items needed to persuade me that not only was my host alive but I was too. I had reached the lobby when I remembered the fine I'd incur if I went out in public. Anyone who broke quarantine, Boris Johnson had recently warned, could expect a £3,000 penalty. Money I definitely did not have – and what would happen if I couldn't pay, would the sum just grow and grow?

I don't know what it is about anxiety. Sometimes it lies down once it's run, leaving you with a powerless and sweaty giant of a creature, and you bury it inside you yet again. This was how I stood after the burial, empty and alone, looking around at the New York-inspired space I couldn't leave. So far I hadn't accepted the enormous lounge's offer to lounge, but now I spread myself on the white ocean of the sofa and tried to think logically. There was no obvious reason for anyone to set a secret agent on me. I was lonely and miserable, emotionally crippled, but I was a good citizen. I had been earning my own money for a long time, and kept my problems private. I had self-destructed with my own consent, entirely in accordance with the law. What would anybody want with me? And even if my host *was* an agent, what had I given him that he couldn't easily obtain by other means? I walked back through my days in the flat, trying to work out what I had given away, but there was next to nothing.

I was still dizzy but no longer frightened when I got up off the sofa to continue my search of the flat. There was nothing to be found in the bedroom either. The drawer in the bedside table was empty. No handkerchiefs, no condoms, no fallen-off button, none of the silly little bits you don't have the heart to throw away, because they remind you of someone or something (a piece snipped out of a local paper, a nice soft stone, an empty pack of cigarettes left by someone you regret having hurt).

In the wardrobe I found three suits and seven shirts; two pairs of trainers, both white. A few T-shirts folded on a shelf. I flipped through them. They were clearly brand new, so it sent a jolt through my fingertips when at last I came across one that was obviously well worn. OXFORD UNIVERSITY, it read. I pulled it over my head and examined myself in the mirror. It was a long time since I'd looked at my face for any reason but to show myself contempt, so it was almost exhilarating to see this OXFORD girl and ask: are you really me, and what is it you've done?

I was still wearing my host's old T-shirt when he let himself in later that night. If it even was his T-shirt, and not merely a prop planted in the flat for depth. By this time I'd considered my options and rejected both fight and flight. All that remained was to play the game as a woman, to submit and hope that in submission would appear a crack, a chink through which I could slip my devilish hand and seize my executioner by the heart.

'Long meeting,' I said, acting hurt and a touch bewildered, the way I've learned men like it, but he only nodded and went straight to the wine fridge, picked out a bottle and held it outstretched to me like a question. I nodded, taking the proffered glass as well, but with a look meant to be read as both accusation and challenge. 'You see how good I look in these clothes?' I asked. I noted a slight curl of the lips, which must have been the onset of an answer, but I cut him off and carried on. 'I missed you, I'll admit it, so I went looking for something of yours, but this place is almost empty. In fact, it's so empty in here I had a crazy thought. I thought you weren't the person you pretend to be. At first I assumed you were a secret agent, but that didn't seem to quite make sense. Then it occurred to me you might be a kind of program, an algorithm, a love code, and I might have been selected as a test subject because of my emptiness. Do you want to hear a story, while I'm baring all? When I was a child, I was terrified my parents had been replaced with robots. I spent most of my time performing secret rituals, trying to work out if they were still human. Funny thing to dread, when you think about it. Why was it worse to imagine robots were inflicting pain on me and on each other than people?'

My host was looking openly, appraisingly at me. What's your game? he seemed to be asking. Then all at once he smiled widely and put his arm around my shoulder. 'You're sweet,' he said, 'but have you heard about the simple living

36

movement? I found out about it five years ago. It's not just possessions. I went through everything. My relationships. My habits. It's about identifying and removing all the things preventing you from achieving the results you want. All the things that drag you down, that sap your energy, you simply cut them out. It's amazing what it's done for my concentration, my ability to perform. Just look around, there's nothing in here I don't know for certain that I need. It brings me tremendous peace. Still, there is something I'd like to get off my chest, since you've been generous enough to share. I do have one habit you might describe as unnecessary. When I meet someone like you, it makes me want to give you my life, because my life is good.'

I don't know whether it was him or me who leaned in first, or if we did it at the same time, but the fact is that we kissed. Hesitantly at first, then fiercely, dog-like, almost fatalistic.

It was my first kiss in six years. I've kept myself to myself, to stop people getting hold of anything to abuse. 'I'm not used to other people, we have to go slowly,' I said, but they were only words. I'd kept myself under house arrest, but never – I understood this now – had I lost the ability to be free.

Anyway, it's a new day, and it's still raining. I'd just got to the part where T and I were on a plane, so that's where I'll pick up.

*

I was so aroused, so frightened on that plane, that I no longer noticed time, or it no longer noticed me. I had no idea how long we'd been flying when I felt a tug in my hip sockets that told me we'd begun to dive.

I remember 'The Winner Takes It All' was playing through the headphones as T, who had a grip on my neck, led me through what must have been an airport and then into a car, which reeked giddyingly of sweat and warm petrol. The engine vibrated in my pelvis. It was extraordinary: the power that had long controlled me turned out at last to be purely mechanical. If I'd been searching for a face behind the violence, a soft spot from which it emerged and could be taken back, I could end my search now. Then the car stopped. T drew me out into the air, which was warm and soft. He guided my feet with his hand, one at a time, up a short set of steps. A shift in the atmosphere told me we were passing through a door, and I sensed it was a large room we had entered. Then, without warning, he let go, and I stood there in my own and Abba's darkness and could barely even tell I was alive. But he came back, leading me into a confined space which jolted into motion, revealing itself to be a lift.

Not until we were in the hotel room did I regain my full senses. T removed the headphones first then peeled the mask back from my eyes. I've tried to remember what I felt, but it's difficult. Something single-stringed and hard, a cold burning metal wire that ran from the nape of my neck to my arsehole, that's the closest I can get. Out of habit I backed towards the bed, where I expected his purpose with me would play out. I was still unsure if he'd prefer a breath-less, little-girlish manner or a vampy arrogance (the third option, the motherly, all-embracing one, I'd ruled out), and I must have been fluctuating weirdly between two faces as I sat on the edge of the bed. T didn't move, only eyed me with his open, sober look.

'I don't want to have sex with you,' he said at last.

'Okay.' I looked at him enquiringly, but it was clear he had no intention of telling me what he did want.

'I can get you anything you like, except for newspapers and magazines. No TV either. You can't pull back the curtains or go onto the balconies. I know you can follow orders. Beyond that, I have no demands.'

'Okay,' I said.

A few minutes later he left, and I was alone. He was right, I can follow orders. If my orders were to be without him and entirely crazed by his absence, then I would carry them out with all my heart's demented skill. I was already pining as I got up off the bed to find some way to pass the time.

I found myself in a suite consisting of three rooms. In one was the bed, large and mournfully pornographic with its velour headboard and gold-painted frame. In the next room you could eat at a dining table or sit on a little group of sofas. I had to edge my way around the room, large as it was, because it was so richly furnished: ornate but empty cabinets, floor vases, candelabras, and a gleaming porcelain puma with bared teeth and a flat spot on its back where there was yet another vase, this one bursting with long-stemmed plastic lilies. In the final room there was a desk and a large oval table, presumably intended for meetings.

Once the initial bemusement faded – I think it lasted about fifteen minutes – I didn't know what to do with myself. I tried sitting at the desk. I'm the president, I thought, altering my stance. I'm a famous, highly regarded author, I thought, but I wasn't sure what the appropriate posture would be, and then the game was over. I took the cap off a fountain pen and slid it back into place. I tried to become interested in a picture on the wall, but it was just the usual small, naked angels and their mother in a cloud – what could I possibly add to that?

Then I decided to take a bath. I've never been into baths, more the opposite really, but I was casting around for an image that would fit the movie I felt I was in, and the whore scrubbing herself in the tub is as iconic as it gets. I was an idiot – I genuinely thought the little basket of soaps and creams they'd set out was the ultimate in luxury. This is what it feels like to be chosen, I thought, emptying the little bottles into the water until it foamed exaggeratedly.

There was almost nothing I wanted more than to be chosen. When an inept school psychologist in Year Six set me the bonkers task of asking my mother whether, if our house was burning down and she had to choose between me and her ghastly husband, she would pick me, she said she

40

wouldn't choose. Even on the psych ward I was hardly ever first choice. There was always someone nuttier, and after a few weeks the doctors started drumming their fingers on the table and wondering how to justify sending me home to make room for someone else. The world had deselected me; I could do none of what it required. I couldn't get an education or hold down a proper job. There was no prospect of me caring for myself long term. I couldn't even hold onto a man. I was unfaithful, I toyed with their hearts, I made them leave, and so they left, and then I was alone with the rent and with myself, an impossible task. There were no signs of improvement, no flashes of promise to remind themselves of the next time I let them down. Social workers, educators, psychologists, psychiatrists, volunteer mentors: they all ran out of patience with me, because I couldn't learn. They needed to feel they were making a difference, at least, given how hard they were working for such a miserable salary. But they weren't making a difference. I was incorrigible. Always extracting new problems from problems that were already myriad.

Now, for once, I had been chosen. It was specifically me T needed. Specifically me he wanted to give all this. Specifically my skills that were required, my fabulous will to destroy.

Day 8

I woke up very early this morning, when it was still dark, and realised I was spooning with my host. It shook me. I tried to lie as still as possible, deferring the moment when he would wake as well, and we would have to seal in words what we had done to one another.

'Hi,' my host said, not long afterwards, reaching for my hand. I didn't turn my face to his, although I felt the impulse. Instead, I asked about the glowing green building outside the window, which stood out among the other glowing skyscrapers. 'That's Lloyd's,' he said, with his lips so close to my neck that I could sense them form the words. 'I did a job for them recently, actually.' My body, lying stock-still, was in tumult, and I listened with only half an ear to his account of Lloyd's Coffee House, which had grown from a gambling den for sailors, shipowners and slavers in the late 1600s into the world's first maritime insurance company.

Half an hour later, I did something I'd have sworn I couldn't do. I sat opposite a man I'd just had sex with and ate a croissant he'd picked up at the bakery as though it were the most natural thing in the world. I had almost let myself get fully carried away when my host suggested I stay a while on the other side of quarantine. That way I'd get to experience the city, and not just from a height. But I found the strength to refuse. It would be crossing a decisive line. I can write about T, but only from this enclosed space. As much as I enjoy my host's company, he must remain the setting around my story.

*

Speaking of T, I'd planned to build up slowly towards the big bang, but I can't stand it any longer – I'm just going to castrate the narrative arc and give the reveal away now: at some point we began to share a large, sharp knife, and agreed that one of us should die. By which I mean: I asked for the biggest knife possible, and he brought it to me. I said: It will lie between us in the bed. We both knew what that meant.

For many years afterwards, I believed the knife was the fulfilment of a prophecy that long predated T's arrival in my life. That the place I occupied in the patriarchy – that of the whore, who plays the role of woman so hard she almost becomes a man – necessarily had to culminate in murder. That both T and the knife were answers to a desire to seal my fate and break with it at last. I'm sure there's an element of truth to that. But one should not underestimate boredom. I see that now. What boredom can drive a person to.

I was bored in that suite. There wasn't a single thing to do. I had my food served on trays, my dirty laundry picked up and returned, all with T as go-between, so that I didn't break the rules and open the door to the outside world. My only job was to come up with things I wanted and could ask T for, but I was soon out of ideas.

I could ask for more shoes, but I'd already asked for ones with plastic heels, ones studded with fake gemstones, ones in gold, ones with platforms, snakeskin, velour, floral-patterned, patent, with bows, with the heel shaped like a flamingo. I could ask for flowers, but I'd asked for all the ones I knew, even those that aren't for sale in shops, red deadnettle and daisies. I had emptied myself of the most absurd wishes. An emerald tiara. A suit of armour. And when I got it . . . it's hard to laugh at your life alone. I didn't even bother trying it on. It ended up in a corner with a tedious Poul Henningsen lamp I'd wanted, because by that time I'd started thinking about resale value.

Anyway, after a while I asked for that knife, and with the knife our relationship blossomed. Until then T had slept on a camp bed in the meeting room. He'd taken considerable trouble to procure a mattress thin enough for his liking. But with the knife we fused, and began to share a bed.

For what felt like ages, neither of us touched it. It lay between us, and was all I thought about. Eventually, one of us might reach for it before falling asleep, and drift off holding the handle. Then we began to scratch each other. At first we scratched our initials, T + D, which spread like some fantastical disease across our bodies. Then one day I was gripped with a furious longing to confess my real name. I was almost dying as I carved a small olivia into his upper arm. He kept his eyes fixed on the knife until the final stroke was made, then took it himself, and I thought he was going to confess as well, but he held my wrist and cut his usual T into my forearm. Then he held my gaze. Had I given him anything crucial by emerging from behind my stage name? Was this real to me now, and still fiction to him? I looked at him steadily as I pushed him down onto the bed. I W K Y, I wrote with our loveknife across his chest. I took my time, put care into each and every letter. Then I bent over him and traced them with my tongue. His blood was in my mouth as I whispered the message into his ear: 'I will kill you.' He smiled, then nodded at the knife. I held my breath as he cut his answer into my thigh. SAME, it said, when I looked down.

Once it's said, it can be said again. I will kill you, I will kill you, we promised one another as the days disappeared around us. There was nothing but the marvellous endpoint and the breathless chase towards it. Those were the days when I began to take him inside me. I did it knowing I had long since run out of minipills. It was wonderful to think of his sperm striving for life inside me, and that I was its master. If those cells had come to me for a name, then they would have one, and that name was death.

Then one morning we woke up and knew it was the day. One of us would die. We could take this no further without making a decision. T left early, as usual (to do what, I didn't know), having eaten his breakfast behind closed doors in the meeting room. I couldn't bear another croissant, not even a cube of melon, so I didn't eat anything. I must have been tense too, I suppose, although by then I'd stopped noticing that sort of thing, living more and more as though I were the knife itself, insensate, a cleaver bisecting a path through infinity.

I spent the morning wondering how to dress for the event ahead. Not overdressed, nor under, I thought, but it's easier to think than to achieve. In the end I settled on a sixties-inspired outfit: a high-necked blouse and miniskirt. But I kept dithering over whether or not to wear tights. On the one hand it was too raw, too direct, to die or kill bare-legged. On the other, I didn't have tights that went with the colour scheme I had going on with the blouse and skirt. If you asked me now whether at that moment I was crazy, I couldn't give you a straight answer. I don't know what I was. I felt clear, empty, holy. As though my head were a majestic bell and death the note I was created to sound.

So why, at the last minute, did I change my mind? I have no idea. I wasn't gripped by a sudden affection for the world. There was no painfully strong bond I realised I could not break. It didn't dawn on me abruptly that I was about to let an anonymous rich man steal my life. It didn't occur to me in a rush how wretched a deity it was I had worshipped. I was simply gripped by the urge to pack. Impelled frantically to scrabble up as many things as I could before it was too late. I only had my wheelie suitcase. Even with just five pairs of shoes and the tiara in there, it was already a struggle finding room for more. Which was more valuable? The designer lamp or the medieval sword? And what about the armour, the bearskin rug, the ermine coat – they were impossible to lug around. I packed and repacked, trying desperately to keep a running total in my head, choosing the items that would make me the most possible cash, until at last, in a fit of temper over all the things I couldn't help but lose, I dumped the contents of the case onto the bed and let all my wishes lie. By the time T walked through the door, I stood ready with my coat and empty case, looking like a typical undergrad on a trip.

'I'd like to go now,' I said.

'Fine by me,' he answered.

Then he opened the meeting-room door, returning moments later with a suitcase stuffed with wads of cash. 'You get one of these,' he said, 'for every day you've been here.' He counted out loud as he took the bundles one by one out of the bottom of the case and put them on the table. 'Forty-six,' he said, finishing his count, and looked up at me. 'There you go.'

Without a word I filled the suitcase with my reward. Then I opened the door onto the world, feeling as I did so that it would be difficult to keep on living without T. 'Good luck,' he simply said, when I turned around to look at him one final time.

Day 10

I did something I've never done before. Last night as we lay in bed, I told my host about T. I was afraid I would be met with judgement, or pity, but there was none of that. First and foremost, my host thought it was a good story. 'Really?' he asked, when I got to the bit with the armour. 'Really,' I replied, and after so many years' delay I finally got to laugh.

I hadn't written all day; it never even crossed my mind. I gazed out of the window at the rain-soaked city; at the Lloyd's building, where my host had performed one of the tasks he did that I would probably never understand. Programming architect? The thought made me smile.

He came home early in the evening with the most beautiful chard I'd ever seen in my life. Large, deep purple and pliant. Taking out a big cast-iron pan (I could have sworn it wasn't in the cupboard the other day, but I must have been blind with fear), he seared the leaves with some beans. The whole thing glistened with oil and honey as he poured it onto two plates.

Then we sat back down at the table, two people who had been close to one another, and it crossed my mind with strange serenity that he, the chard-eater, had had his organ inside me. 'I'm only drinking wine because you're here,' he said. 'Normally I never do.' I sensed it wasn't the truth, but still, I realised he was re-dedicating the habits of his life to me, as if they were in fact new.

We went to bed. It was very beautiful, careful, two systems running delicately through their series of numbers to find the points of connection that had to be there. He fell asleep, his face smoothing out, becoming moon-like, universal. I felt like a bud, an early leaf against the sheet and his quiet nightly body, but then without warning I was seized with fear. I got up with a start and pulled on my jumper. On the balcony I sat down in the rocking egg, which I had previously ignored out of disdain for the concept. I stared up at the greyish-black sky, and found nothing there to hold me back.

*

It's morning now, and I didn't close my eyes all night. My host has left. I didn't try to hide my renewed suspicions, but sent him out the door on a wave of coldness I'm not sure I regret. I'm dazed with exhaustion, I should probably sleep, but the story of T isn't finished.

*

I don't remember leaving the hotel, only that I strode off through a noisy city with my wheelie suitcase. It kept getting stuck on things – a dog's lead, a chair leg – and I was so exasperatedly preoccupied by the inconvenience that I didn't stop to think where I was or where I wanted to go. Onward was my only impulse.

I reached a point where the street led up a long flight of steps. I began angrily lugging my case up them, and had made it halfway when suddenly a man tapped me on the shoulder and reached for the handle. 'NO,' I shrieked at him, and realised only when I saw his startled face that his intention had been to help. 'No,' I repeated in a subdued voice, as the tears welled up. I said it to his back, which was moving swiftly away.

Finally at the top of the steps, I sat down on a bench and cried. They weren't tears of release. They were desert-like and long, and at the end of them stood a person who was myself, staring at me hard-faced. That's how to pull yourself together.

*

With my hardness regained, my focus returned as well. I had to find out where I was. I had to get home with the money as quickly as I could – it was a big risk, staying out in the open with such valuable baggage. Opposite me, on the other side of the path, sat a woman. She was scrolling and scrolling on her iPad and evidently couldn't find what she was looking for. I got up and walked purposefully towards her.

'Excuse me,' I said, 'where are we?'
      'Eeeeeh.' She looked at me in confusion.
      'Geographically. Where are we geographically?'
      'Eeeh.'
      'WHAT PLACE IS THIS?'
      'Eeeh.' She began to get up. 'This . . . is Parco Sempione.'
      'WHAT COUNTRY? CITY NAME?'
      'Milano . . . Italy,' she said softly, starting to back away from me. Then she turned and went off down the path, at the particular pace people use when they're hurrying as fast as they can while also trying not to signal to the potential aggressor that they're fleeing.

So I was in Italy, then. All I had to do was find a train station. I stopped another person and asked for the main station, forgetting to listen to any of the directions except the first one: go straight on. Still, I got there anyway – it wasn't very far, a few kilometres along relatively wide pavements that were easy to navigate with the suitcase.

At the ticket office I had to crack open my bag and hastily snatch out a wad of cash, trying not to let anyone see what an obvious target I was. Just act like a normal person, I told myself when it was my turn to approach the counter. To what extent I succeeded is hard to say, but at any rate I managed to buy a first-class ticket on the overnight train to Munich.

After a few hours' anxious waiting, I was able at last to board the train and lock the door of my compartment. But my calm was short-lived. The conductor had a key, and could easily let himself in while I slept. Taking my bag would be child's play. There was no choice but to stay awake all night. I lay gazing out of the window as Italy became Austria and Austria became Germany. Here and there, lights were lit in human houses. Here and there an IKEA, deserted at night, a petrol station, a lorry followed by two more lorries.

I didn't think about T. I didn't think about the journey I was coming from. If I did, it was only as an undercurrent amid my concerns about being robbed. As long as I'd been paid, I hadn't been humiliated. But what if I lost my fee? It would force me to see what I'd agreed to.

Day 11

It's night in London, and for once the weather is clear, the moon peering down through a light haze of exhaust fumes. Earlier, from the balcony, I saw my host come roller-blading home. His head was a little ball, moving forward in long, elegant thrusts. It reminded me of those funny decorative objects people sometimes have in their homes, where metal balls on strings are made to swing and knock against each other, and for a while they keep each other in motion. Were my host and I those balls? I thought, and couldn't help but feel a certain pleasure. It's true, after all, that we each hang on a string, and occasionally we bump into one another.

I can't love anyone, I told him over dinner (ravioli, freshly shelled peas and walnuts, buttery sauce). I don't know if I'm play-acting. Or rather, I've lost all sense of what my play-acting is meant to convince him of. Most likely I said it to bait him. To make him feel as though he can obtain something no one has obtained before. But only maybe, if he tries very hard.

As we lay in bed – and as usual he had fallen asleep quickly – all at once I was sure he was faking it. I stared at his eyelids, and it was as though they laughed a dry and noiseless laughter.

Now here I sit, and I daren't turn away from the screen. Behind my back, all the time, the sensation of that closed and wakeful laughter.

Day 12

I don't know why I got so upset yesterday. I was so anxious that I did something I really shouldn't have. I went out. Let myself get drenched in the rain which I had only dreamed of from the covered balconies. I saw no police, no suspicious citizens, only a few night-shift workers, round-shouldered, closed around their own bitterness. When I got home and found my host asleep, I forgave him immediately. Even if he was a machine, a manipulative love code, it would need rest too, and maybe even my love.

This is my penultimate day in London. Even now, having put down for the first time what I remember of our trip, I have no clear sense of T. If I'd been hoping I could write his face back into being, crack the shell, re-arrive at my own life, I have disappointed myself. Everything is and remains a strange blur, and I myself a transparent, heartless tourist.

I sold myself, as we all do. Gambled and put everything at stake. I bet everything I had in hopes of winning big. But was that all? Was it just the money I was after, when I accepted T's offer? No. The biggest draw was death.

In this ghostland of little-girl bodies, of mental illness, of abuse, of council offices and shiny shells, in this ghost-land, death was the only thing that could make life real, could speak hatred, could speak pain and terror in clear terms. Death was a reminder of the body, its porosity and dependence, and at the same time the final refusal of it. The last, cruel triumph.

I used to feel a rush of victory when I thought about how every once in a while I probably bumped into a man in Copenhagen I'd had sex with, and didn't even recognise him.

*

You think you can get inside me, but I'm long gone. These chilly rooms you move through are your own. Your dick, your dead-vacant thing, it goes straight through me. What you want, you can get, but once you get it, you understand how very alone you are. I am the devil who reminds you that behind your own face is another, and that too is your own, and that too is deserted.

Such was my revenge. Barren, useless, lonely.

In Milan I chose against death, at least the biological kind. I chose to go home with my suitcase full of money. I thought it was my job to protect it with my life.

And now, soon, I'll be leaving London. Not with a suitcase of money this time but with a short story. It's going to earn me money. I need to ask that of it too, since everything I do must go towards my rent, my bank loans, my food consumption and so on. In that respect it's a good thing the short story is about sex, about a young woman who asks for a knife to kill with and gets it. There's a headline in that, there's a marketable story. I wonder if I'd been aware of that from the beginning, when I first embarked on the journey with T.

My host is busy in the kitchen, risotto with pears. I will turn to him now and to the pears. Perhaps I'll be a different person than I was.

Day 13

Tomorrow I'm leaving London. It feels as though this stay has been my whole life. As though there was nothing before I came here. Earlier today I tried to think of who it was my host had met in Vejle. A person travelling, staying at hotels, who had a stale, dilapidated face. A person lying, incapable of anything else, a person who'd forgotten if there was anything besides manipulation? One thing was certain: he met a person who was lonely. The question is: am I as lonely as when I arrived?

My host came home this afternoon with a necklace. It wasn't as hard to accept it as I would have imagined. I even let him put it around my neck and do up the clasp, as though we were in some silly film. If the gift came at a price, it's not one I'm unable to pay. I want to be the person around whose neck the gold chain is put, as long as I know the deal is temporary. As long as I know that by now, on the thirteenth day, I've given everything I'm going to give, minus a day, or more accurately eighteen hours. After that we will be a beautiful memory, my host and I, a neatly sealed fairy tale I will cherish in my ruined heart the way that children picture tinsel, and not trauma, when they think of Christmas.

*

The story of T is now simply the story of the money he gave me for what I gave him. As I said, I was rattling through

Europe in my overnight compartment, petrified that someone would rob me on the way.

At Munich train station there were flyers everywhere with pictures of three people considered dangerous. Report to the authorities if seen, and do not approach, it said. I stood for ages staring into the pixelated female face, positioned in the centre of the flyer between two male faces that did not interest me in the slightest. What have you done? That was my question to her, the question I could not ask myself. Then I set off struggling towards platform fourteen, my burdensome cargo trundling behind me, to catch the onward train to Hamburg.

All of us are really ghosts, I thought in the compartment, first class, which I shared with lots of suit-clad men who held serious or animated conversations on their phones then typed away at their laptops, feeding into the machine what they had generated, what they had won or lost. I went to get several cups of coffee, bars of chocolate and little bottles of water, which were mine to take; I'd paid for them. I glanced over the newspapers, which were laid out in the same place as the coffee. Most of them had a picture on the front page of an Italian cruise ship lying sideways in the sea. So many Germans, it said in bold red letters, had been on board. Whether they were alive or dead was still unknown.

In Hamburg I circled the station for hours. What was I going to do at home? I could stay in Hamburg, check into a hotel and write the whole story of T, become the writer I had always dreamed of being. But it was the thought of the money that eventually sent me home. It was too unsafe to keep it in a hotel room, where people came and went.

Not until I got my treasure home did I realise I couldn't actually use it for anything at all. You don't just turn up at the bank with a bag full of cash. And if I couldn't put the money in the bank, then I couldn't pay my rent with it either, I couldn't pay off my credit cards or the finance plan on my fridge.

The only thing to do was blow it all. I wouldn't get any pleasure from clothes and shoes, or from expensive and bizarre collectibles; I'd had more than enough of that at the suite in Milan, and the mere thought made me sick. So what to buy? I bought junk food. It's incredibly expensive living off junk food for six months, especially if you can't make up your mind and order far more off the menu than probably any human being can eat in a single sitting. My fridge bulged with saggy nachos, half-eaten cheeseburgers, cold fries. I let them sit for weeks, guilt-ridden, until eventually, with the abrupt determination of self-loathing, I threw the lot into a bin bag to make room for fresh destruction. All my other necessities I bought at the corner shop. I moved along a fairly small axis. My bed to the shop to Selina's Burgerhouse. Then the reminders started piling up: the rent, the electricity, the phone, the DEBT COLLECTION threats. If I hadn't been perpetually drunk, which is also expensive, I would have been afraid.

I called Steffie and apologised repeatedly for my prolonged absence and any trouble it may have caused. She wasn't happy, to put it mildly, but then again I wasn't the first wildly unreliable person she'd dealt with, so she agreed to put me back in the rotation. But when Tuesday came and it was time to go to work, I couldn't budge. It sounds more dramatic than it felt – I just lay in bed, wanting to get up, but couldn't. Ten minutes before my first appointment, I switched off my phone to avoid the barrage of calls from the receptionist at the brothel.

Those days, lying paralysed in bed, I was overcome with grief at losing Anastacia. I longed for her heavy down duvet, to lie with her beneath it. I longed for her arrogant laugh, her heat, her magnificently filthy language. I longed for her clear insight, which, like a cool and unattainable night sky, sharpened and amplified all that she was. I remembered the time when – for a man, at his behest – she'd licked me. But the string of words I cried out as she did so, takeme, takeme, iwantyou, they weren't meant for him. It might be the truly horrifying thing about this story, that. Not the devil-man, not the madness, not the knife, which though it holds sway in my life never touches it at depth. The truly horrifying thing may be the way I've learned to let women fade in the telling of my story, although we were the ones who shared it. Although they were the ones, in fact, who touched me deeply.

At the benefits office they made it clear they were losing patience, but then again they'd been making that clear from the first moment I arrived, so there wasn't much appreciable difference. After a brief conversation, a random person decided that I could not be allowed to keep my

level-three disability rating. I was demoted to a one –
reasonably suitable for work, ready to try – and told to put
three crosses on a screen where every conceivable profes-
sion was apparently listed. The crosses were supposed to go
next to the three professions I could see myself in. Anaes-
thetist, electrical engineer, milliner, I ticked. But when I
told them at the desk I'd finished, I didn't have the bravado
to look them in the eye.

Day 13 – Continued

I just woke up, remembering there's one last thing I should
have said. A few weeks after I got back from Milan, T
cropped back up in the form of a very powerful absence.
It was my period, which didn't come. I knew what that
meant really, but dismissed it. My period, I told myself, was
often erratic. I lingered over the thought, passed the cut-off
for a medical abortion and read vaguely online about the
surgical version. I couldn't conceive of it as anything but a
joke, that something inside me would insist on making the
trip real when I looked back on it only as a foggy comedy.

Nonetheless, I got up one day from my grimy bed and
went to see the doctor. 'You don't have an appointment,'
the receptionist said acidly, but something in my face must
have frightened her or aroused her sympathy, because she
asked me to take a seat in the waiting room anyway.

'Good morning, dear,' the doctor said, as though I were
a child, and it was enough to rouse a sharp desire to be

loved by someone – it could be her, perhaps. 'I think I'm pregnant,' I said, when she asked why I had come. 'You are,' she confirmed, after I'd peed in a cup into which she dipped a small pink strip. 'Congratulations,' she added tentatively, more of a question, addressed not so much to me as to herself, and to the protocols that lay out what a doctor is supposed to do if a person who is obviously too broken-down to love shows up with something inside her which requires exactly that. She was visibly relieved when eventually I broke my silence and said I wanted to be rid of it as soon as possible.

As I lay on the operating table, waiting to float off into anaesthesia, I was thinking this was T's final victory. This was always how he wanted me to die. Defenceless, paralysed, being emptied of the scrap of loveless life he had planted in my middle. Then the anaesthetic began to slow my thoughts. I slipped out from my bitterness into a sucking tunnel of light.

*

I'm going to lie down now beside my host again. Maybe I'll even lie close to him, and he'll register me without waking up. When you love someone, can you ever think back to a moment where you didn't love them yet, or does the way you feel now alter things in retrospect? Perhaps you thought that love would be a convulsion, sending you from one place to another, but when suddenly you love someone, doesn't it feel as though you always have, as though there wasn't any shift at all?

Day 14

I'm leaving today. I was ill at ease and restless when I woke. I tried not to think about whether I wanted to stay. But I did. The prevailing luxury of my host's carefully designed, half-empty home has crept up on me. The time we spend together is very enjoyable, problem-free. How easy would it be to live like this for ever, high up in this distant decadence that is our love?

He'd prepared a lavish breakfast, which we foolishly decided to eat on the balcony. We sat outside, trying to operate a cheese slicer with half-frozen fingers. Still, the advantage of the cold was it explained our silence. We gritted our teeth involuntarily.

Then I sat down to write. All I was missing was a final entry from London, a sort of farewell, but I couldn't concentrate, so I started googling a bit about the devil in literature.

'PERFECT,' I yelled, when I read that Goethe's *Faust* began with a prologue entitled 'Prologue in Heaven'. 'What's perfect?' My host turned away from the kitchen counter and the cleaning-up to share in my excitement. I explained that what I'd been working on for the past fourteen days was actually a short story, in which a narrator in a flat in London tells an old tale about the time that she, like Faust, was tempted by the devil. And this flat in London, much like my host's, was located very high up, almost in the heavens. But I'd been struggling to come up with a title, and now the perfect thing was that the problem was solved. It wouldn't be *Prologue in Heaven*, of course, and *Prelude in a High-Rise* was a bit too odd, but *The Devil in a High-Rise*, just listen to that, I said, waving my arms enthusiastically – isn't that brilliant?

Just like that, I felt ready to go home. I had finished a short story. I had broken the dividing line between my body and another's, left my house arrest, I had a new life ahead of me, and I was grateful to my host for giving me that. But I couldn't be a rich man's wife; my blood began to course more quickly. I didn't need a new prison. 'Could you drive me to the airport right now?' I asked merrily. My host put his mouth very close to my ear. Then he said in a voice I immediately recognised as T's: 'Whatever you want, you shall have.'

*

It's evening now. My plane has taken off. What do I want? If you'd like to know the answer, you'll have to ask T.

Open Houses

i once said
we can't
know
what love is
until we
have abolished
capitalism
but then
you shouldn't
believe everything
i say

*

no
for here i am
eating
my heroic
witless promises
to never
open
my heart
up
again

*

you are happy
you dummy
says my brother
my sister
my beautiful friend
well yes
i'm happy
i've always been happy
only
we live
in a miserable world
where we can't
seem to share
even though
it would be
so easy to

*

what i'm saying
is storm
my house
dear friends
you are within
your rights
just as i
may
live in your houses
if i
promise to

treat you
kindly and
with respect
which i
duly
promise

*

which i
duly promise
though i can't
quite
guarantee
i won't ever
be an idiot
again
in which case
i will have to see
if you'll forgive me
or if
i must go
wandering
after new
houses
but if our houses
are open
then life
is not so bad
not even
for idiots
and idiots

we all
are
of course

*

what i'm saying
is there is a big party
on the horizon
i have already fucked
the devil
and honestly it wasn't
that much fun
so let's create
that something else
which is already here
if only
we give ourselves
to one another

*

oh
the time
i wasted
when i thought
that victory was
stabbing a knife
into oneself
because victory
is quite
bewildering
a jumble that

we make our own

after which we do
everything we can
to share

*

after which we do
everything we can
to share
and bury
deep down
what we should not use
atomic bombs and
those enormous
fishing nets
for those
we should
not use

*

there's a lot we bury
but a little
we keep
for a museum
and when one day we
stand at the museum
and look at the display
of dollars
and kroner
i'll say friends

do you remember
in the old days
the world was beautiful
then too
but money –
or more accurately
a small number of
tyrants –
reigned
that was
some bullshit

*

as we stand
at the display
of dollars
and kroner
i will also
think benignly
of the notes
because despite it all we
once
held them
in our hands
and our hands
give love
even to that which
we hate

*

merely
touching
merely
passing on
and on
that's how
the world lives
that's how
we get the world
to live
because we cannot
help it

*

we must
cultivate
the impulse
to share
to let go
we must
discover it
we do
already
i see for example
nothing
unless you are there
for when you are there
i see
a pheasant and say
look at that

a fucking
pheasant

*

when you are there
i see a party ahead
or more specifically
you are the party
and i'm so beautifully
sat up at the table

*

yes
i am
entirely
yours
but if you
fuck with me
i'll cry
and go elsewhere
to others
because life
is bad
but not
that bad
if our houses
are open
if the food
is ours
to share

*

if our houses
are open
if we genuinely
love each other
why not then
do it
shamelessly

*

what i'm saying is
work for the revolution
just do
whatever you can
we need
our children with us
and our
sick friends
i am coming
like an open wound
you just have to
accept me

*

work for the revolution
and say no
to locker-room banter
we don't want
to hear about your
cleansing bloodbath

what we want
will not be achieved first
and foremost
with the knife
our butcher gave us
on that lovely day
we will turn
and look at the butcher
without recognising him

*

what i'm saying is
work for the revolution
in whatever way
you can
do it every day
in whatever way
you can
there are some
who want to shoot
we need you too
but i want to feed the children
now
and later

*

feed the children
sing to them
now
and later

write poems
for we need
that too

don't
be lonely

not while
we share
the songs as well as
the house

*

and yet
i will always
be a little
lonely
because a word
never quite
means
the same thing
to everyone

but what does it matter
that life is
the most crazed of myriads
if we share
a house

*

if i genuinely love
and i do

i was born that way

i came
and wanted
to belong

to think
that should feel
like so vast
an admission

*

i once said
in front of a large audience
that i wished
i'd never
been born
i said so and
afterwards
i was afraid
that god had
heard me

*

if you're there god
i would like to say
i didn't mean it like that
what i meant was
and i did say
how can i bear to know
that so many people are suffering
so unnecessarily

because
of the tyranny of the few
how can i bear to know
that life is suffering for no good reason
for so many
how
can i
god

*

but then again
we cannot
question god
and expect only
good answers
in the meantime
those people
i was lecturing
they said
what are you
talking about
really
and that
was a good
answer

*

what would i say
if i could go back
to the child
whose triumph it was

like everybody else
to sell herself

you fuck the devil then
i'd say
just get
some money out
of it

but not without
enlisting
in the ranks
without that
it's too difficult

*

without that
it's too difficult
without you
i cannot
live
it is
that simple

*

without you
i cannot live
sisters and brothers and
beautiful friends
you say
i'm happy and i say
not without you

what is this
this is
love poetry
i had thought
or i didn't think it
without you

i want to
radicalise
my love
for the benefit
of the many
i expect
it will go well

*

dear friends
like the idiots
we are
we can find
no fault with
one another
we take it all in
and transform ourselves
together

*

but how dull
it was
back when i had

closed my heart
and thought
i could know
i was safe

i understand now
that
when i had
made myself
quite cold
really i was frying
over the patriarchy's fire

*

sisters and brothers and
beautiful friends
what we have
is very simple
each other and

a muddle of things
that pass from
hand to hand

we will still
be baffled
by the
odds and ends
we have inherited
and the words

the words
thank god can

never be cleansed
for we spoke into them
with our
wonderfully
filthy mouths

mouth
after mouth

in this grimy
transforming portal
we transform together
what we bring

*

listen
our houses
must be open
even to the things
in ourselves
that have been
to that grim
school
we may be
trash
but even trash
can laugh
and when we laugh
we open up
the doors

*

what will i say
to the child
whose triumph it was
to be presented with a butcher's knife
presented with a butcher's knife
by a butcher
who for amusement's sake
wanted to see the child angry

dear child
i will say
if you simply butcher
your butcher
he no doubt
deserved it
but don't think
it will make you
free
it's too hard
to play avenger
if the houses are shut
if you are alone
then you can be sure you'll
never be free

*

i think
this will be the day
i say things quite
frankly

not even my father
would i abolish
not even though
sometimes
when he was drunk
he did not know
the difference between me
and his own
desires

not even him
would i abolish
only
his power

*

come on in now
all of you
did I not say
the party was open

we
may be
trash

but what we really
owe each other
we are in fact
capable of giving

*

coming
like an open
wound
saying things
quite
frankly

it was lonely
in my family
in residential treatment
the group home
section o
and level 6

it was lonely
swallowing
all the pills
lonely
in a couple
being raped

in future
you must
promise me
i won't be
quite myself
because we have
each other

*

listen world
you that are new

i will never
be raped again
and i do want
to love

to think
that that should feel
like so crazy
an admission

*

so crazy
is this song
which begins
with a no
we were not made
for groping

so crazy
is this song
you'd think
we sang it
from another
world

*

that we are
just this
makes us capable
of transforming
what we are

that we are each other
is the oddest
problem

*

in a way
it is very
simple
where there
is violence there
is not
love
because love
is violence's
opposite

*

it quite
simply means
that they
who would
rule
cannot also
claim
to love

remember that
*

remember that
when you consider

who
to go home with
and which houses
you
should leave
at once

*

remember that
when you consider
whether you should
be an anarchist
because quite simply
you believe
in love

*

so what
shall i say
to the butcher child
who asked
about a knife
to butcher with
because it was all
she understood

dear child
here is the knife
use it well
and remember
that my house

is open
if you ever
need
to be held

*

now goodbye
old world
you hatched me
and for that
in spite of everything
you have my thanks

where we now
shall live
i will
shamelessly share
the traumas
you wrote
in my body

where we now
shall live
we must spend a while
listening to what
you wrote
old world
in our bodies

listening and setting
each other free

to live
with one another

*

dear
friends
i have a
pretty big
libido
which will
need putting
into practice

and now that our houses
the party
are open
what i'm saying is
i'm coming
i am yours
that is
for sure

The Devil Speaks from the Madhouse

I arrived at the yellow Renaissance building in an ambulance. Before I got there I'd put on an epic show. I played a woman who was possessed by the devil. I spoke at great length about the time the devil lured me to Milan and planted his seed in me. I said that from this seed had grown a fantastical being, a winged hatred that flapped in my chest. It made a big impression on those around me, and in return they sent me here.

Shortly after I arrived, they fitted an electrical hat I hadn't seen before onto my head, connected via cables to a small, grey, humming machine. I was already quite doped up and pretty slow when this was going on, but nonetheless I was curious about what information might be running from me into the little humming thing. I was hoping I'd be a sensation, something truly misbegotten, but when the results came back the doctor had nothing to report but that my dream centres were active in my waking state. That was that – I was finished being studied this time round, and they gave me an extra diagnosis and a corresponding prescription in reward. Everybody looked away.

*

For months I lay in bed like a corpse. I said nothing, because there was nothing to say in a house where the masters believed they had done away with the devil. I merely opened my medication-heavy hand with difficulty and accepted my pills. Or I sat like a sick plant in my chair, limbs slack, opening and closing my mouth to pretend I was singing along to the song about the budding rose at morning assembly. My life was reduced to a single conflict: my desire to go to bed and the staff's insistence I get up.

Then abruptly, with the arrival of spring, the devil began to grow in me again. It manifested first as a faint but irksome itch under my fingernails. I studied them precisely, found nothing visibly changed, but the nuisance remained. Then came the hot flushes, a heat like the centre of an anthill, dense as an egg. It became impossible to lie still; I paced hurriedly up and down the corridor, waiting anxiously for a message. Then one day in the TV room I found a book someone had left behind, an anatomy book that opened up the human form in layers. I flipped through its pages, distracted and impatient, until suddenly the uterus revealed itself to me in red. I shut my eyes, I could hardly believe it. But it was true. The uterus looked like the head of a goat.

For a while I kept my knowledge to myself. I sat often by the window in my room and let the sunlight kiss my cheeks. I was carrying the downfall, the overthrow, the power of total transformation at my hips, and I couldn't help but smile. Then one day before the dawn, I went to the toilet, and from my arse came the devil's lovely voice: let the words flow.

You locked me in here because you want me to die. Don't try to pretend otherwise. Ever since I was little, you've made it obvious you don't want me. I was sent out of class for being naughty. Sent out of class? I was supposed to disappear, which means to die.

I can't respect anyone who's never sat in a headmaster's office. You have no idea what it's like to be offered a fizzy red drink and absolved of your sins. You have no idea that the price of a little affection is to confess you don't belong. Next time you offer me a fizzy red drink, I'll say no. I realise this will be my downfall, but it will be yours as well.

Why was I sent away from residential treatment, just because I didn't want to eat at the table? Why should I have pretended you were my family, when you could have got a better job tomorrow while I was left behind in your box?

I'm not schizophrenic. I don't have social anxiety. I hate you. It's not a sickness, it's a threat.

When I was seven years old, I started shitting my pants and cutting holes. I cut into everything it was possible to cut. Houseplants, clothes, curtains, even the tea towels in the drawer, I didn't forget about those. The scissors were confiscated, but no one could control my arse. Once, on a school trip, I put a pair of shit-stained underpants at the back of a kitchen cupboard. I was ashamed, and delighted too when everybody started talking about the stench. Later I grew less discreet in my methods. I shat in the sink and left it there. I just wanted to see it, I explained to the grown-ups writing the report.

It destroyed me, you writing those reports. Why did you even look at me if you weren't going to love me? I really hoped you loved me, but when the report was finished I was done.

Then, I began to faint. I passed out in the street. They had me checked for asthma and for epilepsy, stuck a needle in my back – what that was for I don't recall. But there was nothing wrong. I was just being dramatic. I was fantastically large. At night I lay aching in my bunk, because my destiny was bigger than my body.

I used to dream about revenge. I knew that one day I would orchestrate a bloodbath of unheard-of beauty. I ran around alone and pretend-played that I was a horse. I could love that horse, and I suffered with it when it was ailing and couldn't run any more. But I also bored a finger in its side, as though the finger were a spur, and said, Keep going, dummy, all you have is hatred and your long horse legs, and if you don't run fast you're finished.

Even in those days I had to keep everything a secret, and that's why I went mad. Love is people fighting behind closed doors. Society is people fighting in the open but calling war their life. I had to keep all that inside my mouth, because you can't tell the truth without bringing violence on yourself.

When I was ten I switched on all the gas hobs in the kitchen, thinking that at long last it would get me some lives on my conscience. What it got me was another fizzy red drink, and expelled. By that point the reports were so many that they took up more space than I did. My life was enormous, magnificently governmental. I floated like some terrifying clown mask above the paperwork.

I cried only in front of the mirror. That child in the mirror, that child I loved, because she wept in her own tower-room, where nobody could reach her, she wept in her perfect beauty.

If you want to kill me, why are you doing it so slowly?

*

To my fellow devils: are we users? Citizens? Patients? No. If we weren't monsters, we wouldn't be locked up. Our dignity endures only as long as they're afraid of us.

Who was it that told me, when I was living in the group home, that I cost 40,000 a day? My social worker, one of the teachers? I really hoped you'd love me, but it's hard to be worth 40,000. It's hard to be lovable for so great a sum of money every day.

I wouldn't have grown so disgusting if you'd loved me. Why do you think I went around shoving my pussy into the face of any old man I could find? It wasn't that I liked their smell.

Congratulations, you healthy bastards, on not having shit come out of your mouths. I want to live. Do you understand that? Do you understand that what makes me a devil is this simple ambition? I can't shut up about my life. I demand that you carry my words with you.

To those of you who raped me: that's all over! Did you really think I'd sit here gathering dust in my allotted room? I'm coming out, and I'm coming after you. Know this: my fate is also yours. Do you understand what that means? You won't be free until I am. That is what that means.

*

To those of you who think you've done right by me because you paid your taxes, that's all over! First you bury me alive, then you expect me to say thank you. Write up a report. Try to control my arse. It's full of shit, and it will stay that way until I die.

Men are finished.

Taxpayers are finished.

It's not a sickness, me hating you. It's a threat.

Do you remember when you had me intelligence-tested? I thought I would be praised, walking up to the white table to be handed the result. I thought I'd been a good girl. But I was slightly below average, although not brain-damaged, and that's what you were trying to rule out. How did you think I was going to respond?

What did you think I'd do with it, the model of my brain you put up on a board? What if I drew a doodle and said it was your life?

If you'd cut out my tongue, it would have made you dirty, but you left the room in unsoiled white coats. Still I dreamed that you would love me. I admitted I was what you said so that you'd comfort me. But just as I was lying down, you declared I had achieved insight into my symptoms, and could be sent home.

Do you feel disgusting too? Do you also beg for love from those who wish to dominate you? Do they also beg for love, but then will you dominate them? Is the only difference you can see that I'm locked up? I wonder what they're thinking, the passers-by who see me smoking in my cage? They look away, but why? Come back on a day when the ward's only lighter, attached to a chain inside the cage, stops working – then you'll see a person going nuts, a person bawling their eyes out. I have nothing left but an ugly show, but then again it really is ugly, so I think I can squeeze a bit of money out of it.

Even the devil can be pitiful. Even the devil can peer into the glass box where you write up your reports and dream of a hand stroking its back. Even the devil can be conned into thinking it was good once and can be good again, if only you would show it mercy. But then again, the devil isn't stupid! It knows that in the game you've set for it, there are two outcomes: submit or remain a monster. And the devil, which wants to stay alive, can only choose the latter.

Oh no, poor devil that inhabits me. Me, who hungers so appallingly for love that I'll do anything. The other day I texted four different guys, telling them about the extended visiting hours on the weekend. Two of them said they'd come. It sent me into frantic joy immediately replaced by shame at my repulsiveness. The first one came and sat in a chair in my room. I offered him everything, giving him at the same time the impression he meant nothing. We broke the rule about not having sex on the ward, and parted saddened and ashamed.

What would I do if someone loved me? Just meet their eye? I don't think I can do that any more. I'm sorry.

Sorry that I ducked to avoid a loving gaze. Sorry that I bolt towards wherever love is not.

It is a nightmare, this.

I want out.

I don't want more stew.

You want to kill me, yet you don't. This is the limbo you call compassion, social welfare, psychiatry.

*

Many of us are in here because of the patriarchy. Because you people don't know who you are unless you have someone to intelligence-test.

Because our father took his anger out on us, when he wasn't sure that he could force the women he despised to stay with him.

Because he took his anger out on us, because he needed the women he despised, because he couldn't bear his self-contempt alone.

Because he took his anger out on us, because he loved and despised his mother, despised her for letting herself be despised by a man, and vanishing in the way that all who let themselves be despised will vanish.

Because he despised us, because he loved us and realised that one day we'd despise him too.

Because our mother took her anger out on us, because she despised the man she loved because he despised her, because they each despised themselves, that they couldn't be alone in self-contempt and had been forced to choose each other's.

*

Because the child was meant to save her, she despised herself, because the child could not, because the child despised herself, because the child could not help but show to her how hideous, how terrifying love looks when it is defenceless.

I lost my father to love. My mother.

I am very lonely.

Do you hear me?

I am very lonely. I will die of it.

Have you ever thought about how closed your families are? What is it you're protecting? Money? Is it really only that?

I was seven when I began to cut.

Don't tell me yet again to love myself. I cut small-time psychologists to pieces.

*

But first I have to get out of hospital.

I have to get out now.

Listen carefully, Olivia. I am the devil, I can move through anything, but you cannot. I'm going out now, so you know there's somebody to run to when you run. You need me, but you also need friends of flesh and blood.

*

This is how the devil came, and how it left me again, one summer's night just before dawn. I pined desperately in the hours that passed until the contact person that day opened my door and informed me that I was to go to breakfast. The dining room was bathed in sunshine. I took my porridge when it was my turn in the queue, forgetting to say no to fruit compote. It was the compote, thick with sugar and glisteningly red, that I was staring down at when I felt a finger in my side. I turned my head and looked into Erik's widened eyes. 'I have something for you,' he said, and I followed his gaze downward to the table, where he had placed a hundred-kroner note.

Hello sunshine was written on it, and underneath was drawn a big heart. It wasn't the first time Erik had offered me money, but it was the first time I'd accepted, picking up the note and studying his handwriting. 'It's beautiful,'

I said. Erik swilled his glass of juice and grinned slyly. 'I have more.'

Erik comes into money at regular intervals, and it always leads to trouble. Apparently you're not allowed to hand out money on a psychiatric ward, and he refuses to accept that, just as he refuses to take the notes which the staff go to great lengths to recover from the people on whom he has bestowed them.

After the porridge, which both of us simply stirred around, we went out into the cage and smoked. I told him I was planning to run away, that the devil was waiting for me out there, and I hoped a few others would join me. He pointed up at the sky, which was screened from us by a net. 'It's just chicken wire,' he said. 'You can cut it open.' A wave of restlessness rolled through his body – he clenched his jaw and snapped his fingers on both hands, I suppose to emphasise that anything is possible, but only if you act.

'How much money do you actually have?' I asked. Erik leaned towards me, his face very close to mine. 'Do you want it?'

'Yes.'

Then he yanked his baggy jeans down over his hips, stuck his hand into his briefs and took out seven hundred-kroner notes. I stared at the lukewarm money, around which I had instinctively closed my hand. It was hard to decide whether a boundary had been overstepped, and if it had, whether I approved of the transgression. Then I heard the handle turn and stuffed the notes into my pocket.

*

'Do you want to hold hands?' Erik asked a little later, when we were alone once more in the cage.

'No,' I answered, meeting his eye.

'Okay, okay.' He thrust his hips forward and bent a couple of times at the knees. I read a zest for life, an open pain into the movement, whether his or mine I didn't know.

Winter Cabin

it is night
the book is coming
to a close
the farmer has switched off
the electric
light but he forgot
about the moon
that's shining down
on the white tarp
under which the sugar beets
lie stacked
soon they will be taken
to the factory
for every night of frost
the percentage of sugar is reduced
and thus the value of the sugar beet
a whole landscape
may be rendered superfluous
if the bottom line
is red

it is night
my computer
lights up the room
there is news
from parliament
which has assigned
a taskforce
a group of experts
will investigate
the financing behind
scandinavian star
i wonder now if we'll
get answers as to
who owned
the deaths
and if we do
what will we
do about it
if the executioner
looks like the house
where we learned to live

it is night
i'm writing and
behind my words
my child sleeps
in bed
she turns
and murmurs
a dreamword
i wonder if the taskforce
has shone a light into
her dream
i wonder if it transforms
into the blue
swimming hall we know
so well
where the sun
sometimes hammers
in through the big window
i wonder if somewhere
in the blue
she senses
something terrible
i can't
prevent
or which
comes in fact
from me
what do i know of
what my child knows
i know she knows
that she can't really

live
if i can't
love
so i must
love

it is night
and winter
has the summer
in its snow-stilled mouth
just as i
carry my child
on my tongue
yes carry everything
that has abandoned me
there on my tongue
it was winter too the night
i birthed my child
i held her close to me
my stranger-self
she cried about it
i said
there there
you have to live
with me
bringing you
into the world
and condemning you
to live
off me

it is night
the frantic
pheasant screams
i tell myself
that it's about the cage
where it was born
and came
to know itself
like the heat
of a heat lamp
later
it was put outside
but only so that later still
it could be shot
but for now
its heart is warm
and keeps
a secret
over which
no one is master

it is night
the book is coming
to a close
venus is shining
very brightly
and my computer
has also learned
to shine
in a comment thread
the other day
someone wrote
that it's absurd
how insurance companies
can quantify
what life is worth
just like that
and in response a person
by the name of bent
wrote
that's just
the way the world
is made
but there
bent is mistaken
there is nothing made
we can't
unmake
if we want to and
there are enough of us

it is night
the cabin winces
in the frost
the woodwork
contracts
awaiting the thaw
the expansion anew
i hear
the bed creak
in the room
on the other side
of the wall
it is my
beautiful friend
turning
in her sleep
she is never
only one
now especially
she is two
because she has a child
beneath the skin
which turns
with her

it is night
but earlier
it was day
we went across the field
frost-bound and wide
along the dank
stream
where pesticides run
wastewater runs
the sun hangs
red and beautiful
so low
above the horizon
gusty
but the windmills
stood
as so often
still
because
of some financial
technicality
i saw her
my beautiful friend
in that harrowed
and living
landscape
and asked if i
should take a picture
where she was
in front of the sun
yes

she said
i took three
apparently i needed
a device
to say
i see you
and i'd like to
give you
back the beauty that i see
although i do know
how it is
with beauty
you are always left
with something in your hands
you need
to keep

it is night
my friend
has a child beneath the skin
and beneath my child is me
and countless others
for to love my child
i must love others too
so i do
love
that something else
i have
in my heart
'mama'
i hear suddenly
from the bed
'is it morning'
'no sweetheart
it's still night
i'm just sitting here
finishing
this book'

it is night
but no longer
dark and dense
as in a mother's belly
because now the farmer's
machines are switched on
the field
looks very empty
displayed
in the floodlight
a person shouts
something to someone else
and above them venus shines
lucifer bringer of light
who said
that not even
for god
shall you sacrifice your child
your animal love
shall hold sway
this earthly
lunacy
belonging to
the earth

it is night
and the moon
has moved
around the cabin
outside my window now
large and radioactive
beaming
does it not know
about the billionaires
who dream themselves up
to its heights
i think
it would laugh
if it heard
about a man called jeff
'jeff' it would laugh
'is that really
a name
did you really
come up with that
yourselves?'

it is night
and in the night
the farmer's machines
the moon above
the seasonal workers
my sleeping friend
and my child
who beneath the skin
carries me
she owes me nothing
only she is condemned
to carry
me and countless others
yesterday she asked
if we believed in god
and i had to tell her
that i could not say
for sure
if she did or not
'why?'
'well sweetheart
we are not entirely
the same'

it is night
and we are not
entirely
the same
that news
was obviously easy
for my child
she turned back
to her game
and totally forgot
it seemed
the part of her question
that concerned god
but now
i'm ready to answer
that for my part
i don't believe
there's anybody
out there in the sky
who in his
heavenly peace
decided suddenly
to act
no, there was never
only one
but always
countless
that something else
in my heart
that wants out
of itself

it is night
the night contains
a morning
but for now
i put it off
with my frost-clear
nightpoems
the computer lights up
with the taskforce
i wonder if we will get answers
as to who owned the deaths
and what will the truth
do
with itself
if we are ready
to swallow it
because it looks like
the trough
we must eat from
every day

it is night
a few hundred thousand
that's what they were paid
for their dead children
those who came out of the fire
with dreadfully
empty hands
what should they do
with their dirty money
there is no sea
that does not reek
there is no water
that can wash them clean
and so we must go
to the houses of the arsonists
and demand
that they come out
to you who start fires
to you who steal lives
your time is past
and the book
is done

Thank you to Morten for being an indispensable reader and friend, and particular thanks for appealing to my courage during a temporary period of good behaviour.

Thank you to Eini for reading with all the love and strength you have. It made it easier to choose.

Thank you to Anders, Ly and Ursula for being kind enough to house me when I had to finish the book and couldn't do it alone.

Thank you to my friends and siblings for making life liveable – it would be difficult to write otherwise.

Thank you to my child, whose special wish it was that readers of this book should know her name is Isa. Your wish is hereby granted, and thank you to you, my darling, for teaching me life all over again.

SCANDINAVIAN STAR